I0626818

THE VERMIN SLEEP

by James M. Watjen

Nightmare Press
Shepherdsville, KY

THE VERMIN SLEEP

Haunted by a traumatic childhood with an abusive father and a mother's death, Alex Fulmer, struggles to find his footing in life while targeting pedophiles scattered throughout Chicago. Alex eventually lands the job of his dreams as a set builder on a children's television show. Everything seems to be going great until he discovers a director's sinister intentions towards a child actor and becomes entangled in a dangerous game of vigilante justice – a game that could lead him into the horrors he knew as a child, and into the pit of the vermin he despises.

Edited by Jacob Floyd
Cover Art by James Watjen

Thank you for reading! If you like the book, please leave a review on Amazon and Goodreads. Reviews help authors and publishers spread the word.

To keep up with more Nightmare Press news, visit us at:

Nightmarepress.net
Facebook
X
Instagram
Threads
Bluesky
Slasher
Nightmare Press Network on YouTube

To interact with authors and other readers, join the Nightmare Press Fans & Authors group on Facebook

To my family & friends, your love and support will never be forgotten.

Stay weird!

THE VERMIN SLEEP

by James M. Watjen

CHAPTER ONE

It's ironic that a bastard who lived a life tormenting others looks so peaceful. I don't understand, after all these years, how he can lie there so fragile, blank, and stale. His actions have been anything but those. His ability to shape and mold horrific scenes behind closed doors are now lost to time and hopefully Hell, too. The world was oblivious. His friends: oblivious. His co-workers: oblivious. Our external family: unconcerned. All of them were too busy with their own personal shit-shows to realize the nightmare he was unleashing right under their noses. Two feet under their noses. No matter the amount of pain he set loose on this world, he still gets to rest. It's not fair. None of it. Throw the dirt on the son-of-a-bitch. Time stops for no man. Not even the Old Bastard.

Understand the Old Bastard grew up in a neck of the woods where being spoken to meant keeping your mouth shut. You didn't speak. You listened. His ability to remain silent in tense situations accompanied by his ability to hear the slightest gust of wind added to his horrifying persona. He had lots to say but chose other means of communication to make sure his intentions were clear.

Coming from a home that held to the highest of heavenly standards, he quickly learned the church held no affinity to a bastard. His parents had been saved after realizing the church was the one place that would accept them, or their money at least. His relationship with any sort of God would eventually lead him to become the Devil he was.

My grandparents, who were deceased before I came into the world, were well-off from southern drug money: tobacco farms. They came from a lengthy line of slave owners and demanded only proper manners and adherence to the Good Book. A book the Old Bastard would end up keeping at his bedside until his end.

The bastard they called my father was less of the latter and more of a hollow shell with a propensity to indulge in the nightlife. Eager to exit the divinity of his upbringing, he left home at an early age to seek work in Chicago where we took up residence. It was here he spent countless nights tipping the bottle and visiting strip clubs to curb his hunger for violence and abuse. An existence he would only briefly cease and then return to after I made my earthly appearance. Though this was before my existence, I was informed by the one constant that reminded me that kindness still existed: my mother.

The irony of the Old Bastard's beastly being is that he was able to find an angel like my mother. Whether it was the eight-year age difference – my dad being twenty-six and my mother being eighteen when they first met – or a "higher" calling that brought them together will never be known. The details of their first meeting are forever lost, or clouded by the years of abuse I endured after my mother departed this hell. Regardless, the story of *Beauty and the Beast* was a reality.

My mother, Janet, was a beautiful soul. She was a simple woman, who rarely had time to tend to herself. She would throw her long brown hair back into a ponytail, only to keep her vision clear for cleaning, and in the late evenings, watching for the bastard. She was a stay-at-home mother, but for the early 1980s, she was recognized as simply a mother. She resolved to spend time with me and make sure that all the necessary needs were met. Her ability to find good in every situation was a defining factor in her character. If only you could have met her. If only the Old Bastard hadn't driven her to break.

My mother would endure daily hazing when my father had finished his last sip of whatever cheap bottle he picked up from the liquor store. The torment would come in either a verbal lashing or through an intoxicated fury of spit and fists. His cruelty only subsided when my mother would be clinching the floor and pleading for him to stop. The beast would only relent when he was drained of any physical capability and retire to the bedroom. Through all the blood and bruises left from the beatings, she would still have the ability to smile at me, masking the unbearable pain she had endured. I was powerless to defend her and the raging fire this built inside would burn for the rest of my days.

It was near the end of the summer of 1985, when the beautiful soul known as my mother, became ill. At the age of eight years old, I was left to care for my mother as the alcohol had driven the return of the Old Bastard to his true form. Until that summer, he had spent the previous six months visiting a local recovery center, but soon found his repressed urge for spirits became too much. My mother had been feeling ill for some time, and eventually decided to visit the local clinic. There she received the kind of terrible news that felt like it belonged to the pages of a Stephen King novel. She was battling a form of cancer that had no cure. No relief. No happy ending. As soon as the Old Bastard had to begin taking on the additional responsibilities of being a father figure, he folded into the monster I would soon loathe.

THE VERMIN SLEEP

As my mother lay bedridden, fighting the toughest battle of her life, the Old Bastard began frequenting his old haunts and laying the groundwork for what would become my own personal hell for the next fifteen months. He would return at night, laying waste to anything not bolted to the floors or walls. During one attempt to calm him and not bother my mother, I was met with a blow to the head that would sit even the most seasoned boxer on his ass. His wedding ring left a mark that would stain my skin, bruised, for at least a week. It was not the first time incidents like that had occurred and certainly not the last.

The final months my mother spent in my care were some of the most difficult times, yet they formed a bond between us that had grown as strong as any we had known. She would listen to my ideas, my concerns, and my love of all things' theater. I only ever told her I was becoming infatuated with the various shows on television that depicted a world where the horrors of the Old Bastard didn't exist. Shows where children lived care-free and with a loving and nuclear-style family. No alcohol. No late-night beatings. No abuse. We would spend the last of her days watching these shows and escaping into the world we wished we had.

She may not have been as interested in the shows as I was, but she never made it apparent. She would fight through the coughs and laugh right along as we watched the goody antics of the characters. She had become so accustomed to hiding her true self to please those around her, that she made me believe she enjoyed the shows. Maybe it wasn't the shows but the time we spent together that brought her so much joy and laughter. These times of joy would not last forever and I felt the climax of our time together approaching.

4

As the scene ended in our real-world situation, I knew these shows weren't possible for us. My mother was nearing her closing credits, and I had no way to provide a second episode for her. This is what made her passing so difficult. The loss of an earthly being meant for a higher calling than our world could provide. More than *I* could provide.

The day of my mother's passing was worse than I had ever anticipated. I told myself that at the age of eight, I would be able to manage and facilitate life after losing her. Little did I know, the bastard would not let that happen. The day of my sweet mother's passing, the Old Bastard chose to seek comfort in a fifth of the cheapest whiskey he could find and pass out. When he awoke and discovered what he was searching for was not at the bottom of the bottle, he moved to the next one. The Old Bastard was unstoppable. He consumed without regard to his own well-being and felt no empathy for anyone else. As I stood by my mother's bedside, grieving what was the last bastion of love and hope in my life, the Old Bastard sought refuge on the couch, where he slept for the next two days. A bastard to those living and more so to those deceased.

Janet Louise Felmer was laid to rest on a Friday afternoon. Though the sun was bright in the sky, I could not escape the cloud that followed me from that day forward. The eight years of my existence at that point always had a bright ray of sun breaking through the clouds. Now, the sun had spent its fuel, and I was left to search for a new light. A new form of refuge. The funeral had very few attendees, as the Old Bastard had not allowed my mother to pursue interests or friends outside of our home. She was tasked to simply raise me and tend to his needs when summoned.

THE VERMIN SLEEP

The entire time I stood staring at the casket, my father wept in the most disingenuous fashion. Or maybe it was genuine. I had never seen him weep. Never saw a tear before that day leave his eyes. As we stood there listening to the priest give his reading while watching the casket lower, a deep sense of dread overcame me. Once the casket had reached the six-foot drop, I knew the comfort I had previously known was gone. My eyes began to twitch with anxiety. The darkness I felt became a reality much quicker than I expected. Much darker than I expected. Total darkness.

Following my mother's departure from this world, I resolved to keep myself busy with the same television shows that previously brought me so much escape. Hours upon hours of absorbing children's shows in an effort to keep out of sight and out of mind of the Old Bastard. The first few months seemed to pass as if they were only hours. I'm not sure if the company of the television strobe was hypnotizing me or if I was oblivious to the structure of time.

In spite of time passing quickly in those first months, I rarely had contact with the Old Bastard as he would spend his days working on the factory floor, where he cast dies for equipment and hardware. In the evenings, it wasn't unusual for him to arrive with a bottle in hand and migrate to the basement. I never ventured there. As long as he kept to himself in the confines of the cellar and myself in my room, I avoided him. As the days grew on, his routine became more predictable. Wake, work, liquor store, basement. If he was eating, I never saw it and had no intent on sharing a meal, for my own safety.

Then, after months of the same routine, it stopped. The initial morning and midday routine was the same, but now he wasn't going directly to the basement. He would, instead, choose to pour his bottle in the kitchen and proceed to the living room. After taking up residence in the recliner, he would slowly sip his drink and smile. The kind of smile that tells you whatever he was doing was finished. Whatever he was working on had reached its finale. A proud bastard. An Old Bastard.

THE VERMIN SLEEP

CHAPTER TWO

After the Old Bastard realized the sight of me reminded him of things he had lost, my bedroom was moved to a small concrete room in the corner of the cellar. This had been his project during those nights spent harassing whiskey bottles and tooling special mounts at work.

The corner of our cellar became a small room with bare concrete floors, a heavy sliding door, and a single overhead work light. The sight of the room boiled up the fear every eight-year-old faces: the silent and total darkness. A darkness in a room where I would eventually spend hundreds of sleepless nights.

As the fall began to shift and welcome the frozen air of the Great Lakes, the temperature in our home dropped. The air in my new chamber began to reflect conditions outside. School started closing early due to the enormous amounts of snow hindering the buses. It was a miracle the Old Bastard was able to bring himself to roll out of bed and make it to and from work every day without impacting his extracurricular activities. I would continue to spend my time during school closings glued to children's shows and reading the occasional *Zoobook*. My mother had bought a several years' subscription before her passing, and like the children's shows, it gave me a sense of comfort reading about the animals beyond my own world. Sadly, my comfort was short-lived. The cellar room was not what I thought it to be. The initial feeling of comfort from the beast upstairs soon gave way to total isolation from the rest of the world. A sense of loneliness and anxiety crept over me, drawing me into a state of mind of which I was not previously aware: a state of paranoia.

It was during a snowstorm that lead to the weeklong canceling of school that I would learn the Old Bastard's true intentions. After lying down in my bed for the evening, I could hear the Old Bastard stumble down the stairwell and shuffle slowly towards the cellar room door.

"Wake up! You're not going to sleep yet!"

Half dazed from the onset of sleep, I wiped my eyes and spotted the obscured figure standing in the doorway.

"You've still got shit to clean up in the kitchen!"

I didn't know what he was talking about, but I was in no condition for a confrontation. His drunk hands knew no mercy and I had felt the wrath too many times to know when and when not to plead my case. I rose slowly and approached the door, aware that the potential for a beating was standing in the doorway. A darkened figure with shit for brains and bourbon on his breath.

"Move it! I thought I told you to take care of this shit before I got home from work!"

I nodded and continued past as quickly as I could.

The Old Bastard followed closely behind and up the stairs to the doorway. "Clean it up and come back downstairs when you're finished!"

I wasted no time combing over any item that was out of place and made sure there wasn't as much as a crumb left anywhere on the floor.

"Hurry up!"

The Old Bastard had a knack for being an expert in timekeeping, so I knew the consequences of keeping him waiting. I rushed back down the stairs as if the only opportunity at safety was in the promptness of my return.

THE VERMIN SLEEP

The Old Bastard was already waiting. "Get in!".

I entered the cellar room, knowing that any slight against his command would end in torment that would undoubtedly haunt the rest of my life.

He slammed the sliding door shut plunging the room into total darkness. I could hear some commotion coming from the other side of the door.

"Wha...What is going on?"

The sound of a metal mechanism being clinched shut rang out in the emptiness of the cellar. This was the moment I knew the chamber would be my new dark and damp living quarters.

The Old Bastard said nothing, but the shadow cast from outside the heavy sliding door grew smaller, followed by the sound of footsteps stumbling up the stairs.

I knew trying to make noise to get someone's attention that evening would result in more trouble, so in an effort to prevent that, I made the choice to attempt sleep.

Through the entire first night, I could hear the sound of small feet scurrying on the cold concrete floor. The only comfort I felt was that my twin-sized bed was elevated. All night, the sounds of rapid tiny steps pierced my attempts to sleep. I knew what made those sounds. They were rats running across the floor, looking for an exit from the chamber. I had seen them when I first moved into my room.

The next morning, light peered from down the basement steps and underneath the chamber door. I was unaware of the time. I had been unable to move all my belongings to the cellar, and my clock was still resting upstairs.

After waiting for several hours, I yelled out to see if the Old Bastard was still home. No response. I seized the moment and tried to open the door, and realized the sound I heard the night before was a lock being secured to prevent my escape. An intense sense of claustrophobia I had never endured before draped over me as dread became a reality. There was no leaving the chamber. My room was a container for all that which the Old Bastard despised.

I decided to read a few of the *Zoobooks* I brought down to try to forget the hunger that was eating my stomach. After spending an unknown amount of time in the chamber, a silhouette moved closer to the door.

"Your food's done." The Old Bastard slid open the door and slipped a microwaveable dinner into the doorway.

I scrambled to the food as quickly as I could so the Old Bastard wouldn't rob me of my opportunity. When I took the meal, he leaned in and dropped a bucket into the chamber.

I looked at him with a questioned stare.

"Here's your bathroom." He slammed the sliding door shut and shuffled back up the stairwell, his silhouette disappearing from the light underneath the door.

Then darkness.

I ate my food with such tenacity that my stomach immediately bloated.

After finishing my meal, I lay in bed, staring at the ceiling and wondering when the door would grant me an opportunity at escape. The Old Bastard knew I would try and wouldn't let me go willingly. The nickname I gave him he had now earned.

THE VERMIN SLEEP

CHAPTER THREE

The days and nights I sat inside the Old Bastard's chamber fell together. The only moment of time I realized it was day was when he brought food and water. For those brief moments, I knew the outside world still existed.

To keep track of the times the door opened for feedings, I would make tears on the outside of my *Zoobook*. The one with the tiger on the front cover. At this rate, I was fast approaching ten tears. Then it was twenty. Then thirty. Time for another book. I figured it was only a matter of time before someone would come looking for me. I knew my classmates and teacher at school would start questioning my whereabouts. But how long would that be? What was the Old Bastard telling them? Or was he even concerned with that? Given that his love for alcohol would blind him to logic, I decided it was safer to wait it out rather than try to run and face the lashings that would follow if I failed to escape.

Every night, the rats would carry off any remaining pieces of my dinner. I started to grow accustomed to seeing them wait for me to get into my bed so they could grab and devour the leftovers.

One night, in an attempt to befriend one, I offered a piece of soggy bread, only to be met with a small bite mark on my right index finger. The bastards. They only wanted to take and give nothing. They quickly became a reminder that the Old Bastard was still around and any attempt to fix my problems would be met with aggression.

They were quickly multiplying at night. The sounds were getting louder and the hissing and fighting for food would keep me awake for hours. I quickly started to realize the lack of sleep was getting to me. The rats had to be dealt with or I would never rest. Never rest inside this Old Bastard's chamber. I could never sleep till the vermin sleep. For good.

It all culminated in a brilliant plan I devised that lead to a nightmare which still haunts me. My plan was that one evening, after the Old Bastard left the food in the doorway, to lure the rats out and begin smashing them. Smashing them till they all slept the long sleep. The plan was set.

I waited for the Old Bastard to bring the food in and slam the door shut. I knew if I didn't move immediately, the rats would take the food and vanish. I grabbed the food up and sat in my bed. I started throwing pieces down and waited. One by one, they went for the food and I would smash them with my shoe, slamming my foot down as hard as possible. The vermin were departing the world in multitudes, and I was getting closer to sleep. After what felt like hours, I could no longer hear the sound of scattering. No sound of hissing or fighting. The plan had succeeded as I had hoped.

The sleep. It was unlike anything I had ever felt. A sense of solitude and, if for a brief and uninterrupted moment, peace. A peace that would soon end when the Old Bastard returned.

Upon waking, I noticed the remains from the rats were scattered all over the floor. Bones. Brains. Guts. All of it. The dim reflection of the work-light beamed off the pools of blood that lay all over the floor.

THE VERMIN SLEEP

I sat there in my bed, unsure of how I would make this mess disappear. Without time to react, the ominous shuffle and eerie silhouette appeared.

I froze. There was no escaping the inevitable backlash I would soon face from the Old Bastard.

The door slid open. There stood the Old Bastard with another microwave meal. "What the fuck!? You're going to clean this shit up!"

I said nothing, just stared. My fight, flight or freeze response had chosen the safest route.

"You know what? Are you hungry?"

I nodded.

"Well, eat up!" The Old Bastard pointed to the ground and at the crushed rat remains. "You get hungry enough, you'll eat!"

The door slammed shut.

In a last ditch attempt to reassure myself he was the monster he always presented himself to be, I waited. The light under the sliding door went dark. The Old Bastard was everything I thought him to be and more. Not a man, but a monster. The Old Bastard was a monster.

That evening, I barely slept as I hoped that I was wrong. I wasn't. The next day when the Old Bastard opened the sliding door, he was holding only a jug of water, which he placed on the ground.

"Full yet? You will be by the time these damn things are gone." He slammed the sliding door shut, laughing to himself.

After that, the visits to the chamber became less frequent, and my hunger grew uncontrollable. I was left with no choice. I knew if I didn't eat something, he would let me starve.

I made the decision to take the pieces from the days-old rats lying on the floor. The smell was rancid. I grabbed a piece in one hand and my nose clinched in the other. I chewed as quickly as possible, just to get it into my stomach. Several more pieces. Gagging as the vermin meat slid down my throat.

I eventually reached the point where I could not devour another piece. My stomach and my mind had reached their limits. I lay on my bed, clutching my stomach, and closed my eyes. I hoped to wake up to discover everything had been a terrible nightmare. But soon realized I was asleep in the belly of a beast—or at least, in his chamber.

That night I tossed and turned, waiting for the rat meat to make its unwelcome return. By some unknown power, I was able to keep the meat down and drank copious amounts of water to ease any additional hunger pains.

The next visit, the Old Bastard seemed so proud. "Well, looks like you ate a bit! Let me cook you the rest up. We can't be wasting good meat!" He grabbed a shovel from around the corner and with gloves, moved the meat into Ziploc bags. "You've got a few weeks of food in here. I'll bring you some back down later."

I wanted to bash him with anything I could get my hands on, but I knew I would eat far worse if he managed to stop me. So instead, I stared at the ceiling as he finished cleaning up the rest of the rats' corpses. The smell reached an intolerable level and I welcomed any relief.

He finished and slammed the door shut. Maybe it was from the lack of air holding my breath, but I passed out. The past few days had taken its toll on my well-being and the sweet relief of sleep was calling my name.

The following weeks, I ate nothing but the leftover rat meat for dinner. I would manage to down small slivers of the fried meat, a taste I have never forgotten—gamey and still left with parcels of skin and the occasional hair, which I would pull from the back of my throat. During this time, I drank every drop of water given to me. If I couldn't finish the meat, I would resolve to drink copious amounts of water to prevent myself from falling to hunger pains.

I knew the Old Bastard was getting a kick out of returning every night to gather my leftovers. He would make comments trying to entice me to devour more, but I would not let him have the enjoyment of seeing me take another bite. The stench of his alcohol-ridden breath coupled with his demeanor was enough to kill one's appetite.

I knew if I could just stay alive in here someone would eventually realize I was not at school. Eventually, that day would come.

CHAPTER FOUR

I can't remember how many *Zoobooks* I had torn into before the day the police showed up. All I know is I had completely marked the Tiger and Turtle covers with small tears.

As I slept peacefully, I awoke to the sound of multiple footsteps scrambling down into the cellar, and a blinding light growing stronger as it approached the bottom of the chamber door.

"Chicago PD! Anyone down here!"

I hesitated because the thought of the Old Bastard trying to trick me was too strong.

Again, the shouts grew louder. Then, I heard them notice the chamber door and the lock that kept it shut.

I stood up quickly and mumbled, "Hello?"

The police began searching for a way to remove the lock from the door as quickly as possible. "We got someone down here! I think it's the Felmer boy!" The sound of metal beating on metal, as the police pounding the door with their heavy flashlights, never sounded so beautiful.

The police continued to pry the latch and lock away from each other. Eventually, as if some angel had appeared, a bright light pierced the dim lights of the chamber and pointed directly at my face.

"It's the Felmer boy! He's alive!"

Leaving the chamber was a shock to my senses. I was told I had been missing for the last seven months. Seven months of torture and sensory deprivation. As if I was suffering from Stockholm Syndrome, I asked the officer where the Old Bastard was. They told me he had been arrested on multiple charges and assured me I was safe now.

As we climbed the stairs to the cellar doorway and out through the kitchen, I made note of the countless empty bottles of various alcohol brands scattered all through the house. The cowardly Old Bastard was hoping the alcohol would get him before the police; he was wrong.

When I reached the door, I was surprised to see the local news crews and paramedics outside waiting to see me. I was slowly taken to the ambulance where the paramedic deemed I was too malnourished to bypass the hospital.

As I lay on a stretcher outside the ambulance, I looked over to the police car that held the Old Bastard. That look: The look of a creature once human being led away to rot in a chamber, knowing there was no escape. He stared with no emotion. No empathy for anyone or anything; not even himself.

The police car pulled away and I was stretchered into the ambulance.

It was a short drive to the hospital where I would receive treatment via IV. As the investigator strolled into my room, I couldn't hold back from asking him how they had found me. The investigator said when the police received a call from the school about my whereabouts, they went to investigate. The Old Bastard tried to convince the cops that the family who lived there had moved and he was a new tenant. The police grew suspicious of a family moving away from Chicago in the dead of winter, so they pressed more questions. The Old Bastard had said the family moved months ago and had all their belongings shipped out and mail changed to the new address. This is where my mother would once again be the angel of grace. In the Old Bastard's drunken blabbering, he failed to check the mailbox. The officer noticed a magazine hanging slightly out of the mail next to the door: A *Zoobook* addressed to a one Janet L Felmer.

Upon noticing the details of the Old Bastard not adding up and his inability to properly piece together sentences, a call was made to the judge requesting a search warrant. The investigator said the Old Bastard was calm until they went to open the cellar door. He became irrational and yelled for the police to leave immediately, but it was too late. After a small skirmish, the police were able to cuff and seat him in the car while they worked to gain access to the chamber. As if out of some sort of newspaper article, I had been found. Alive. Barely. After being questioned by the investigator and presenting all the gory details of the last seven months, I knew it was time to rest. I laid my head down on the clean hospital bed, closed my eyes, and dreamed of nothing. The first time in seven long months; I dreamed of total darkness and nothing more. It was the most beautiful nothing I had ever experienced.

After several days in the hospital working to gain my strength back, I was released into the care of my aunt and uncle. It had been so long since I had seen them but was welcomed into their home with open arms. Time began passing much more quickly outside the chamber and before I had a chance to realize, I was no longer an adolescent but instead a young man. The years spent with my aunt and uncle were like something out of a movie. I enjoyed the time I spent there but always had the uneasy feeling something was coming in the night. It was as if the Old Bastard's living ghost was following me. I knew he was imprisoned and locked behind tons of concrete and steel, but that never made it easier.

Sleeping had become a struggle and any time I would hear something move in the night, I was instantly transported back to the chamber. I would hear the sound of the vermin creeping along the walls and under the bed. Waiting for me to step foot out onto the floor.

These are the vermin that never slept.

CHAPTER FIVE

As time passed further from my days of the Old Bastard and the chamber, I worked to remove myself entirely from that existence.

The school I began attending was in the suburbs of Chicago. I started spending time with the school's theater club and learning the trade of set design. This was a skill that would not have been fathomable while attending my school in the city limits, so I took full advantage of it.

A core memory I was unable to escape was my love for the children's television shows that had offered me shelter in that hostile environment.

I soon embraced my love for theater and frequented the rehearsals and workshops the school provided. I could not get enough of it. I watched and learned as the students in the set design team were able to craft amazing backdrops. This period in my life helped strengthen my ability to communicate with people and control any fears I would later experience. Eventually, the theater teacher noticed the presentation of the sets is what most interested me. She invited me to join the theater club and from there I grew.

The other kids involved in the theater club were very accepting. Several of them even invited me to be a part of their lunch gatherings. Coming from the hell that was the chamber, the newfound bond I began forming was something completely new to me. It was one of the grandest times of my life. I would continue to frequent the theater club for months, honing my craft as a set designer. Spending countless hours with a hammer in one hand and a nail in the other. It was here that I learned the proper way to drive a nail and the technique to swing a hammer so that every strike landed on its intended target.

One of the other kids, a junior named Michael, quickly saw my interest in elevating my craft. "You really like this stuff, huh?" were the first words he ever muttered to me.

I responded with a nod and continued prepping the set for our next school play: a rendition of the classic tale of Alice in Wonderland.

"You're pretty good with that hammer. You build a lot outside of the club?"

I didn't know what to say as growing up with the Old Bastard made me timid to continue in any sort of small talk.

"Yes, sir." I remember having difficulty properly conveying anything verbally.

"You don't have to call me sir! I'm not that special." He laughed and posted his hand on my shoulder as to give me confidence with the next swing of my hammer.

Over the course of the next month, Michael continued to help guide me in the proper way to construct sets and assist me in building the skills I would eventually use in the outside world.

As time went on, I grew to appreciate the guidance and respect Michael had for the world of theater. His attention to detail and ability to provide feedback in a manner that was less than harsh helped strengthen my sense of self-worth. This is the first time, and potentially last time, in my life that I recall feeling like I was not a loner. I was part of something bigger. I was part of an actual team.

This feeling would continue to the end of the scheduled showings *of Alice in Wonderland*. I received regular compliments from the teacher, as well as Michael. Positive feedback was new to me. I had spent years being physically and verbally abused by the Old Bastard and wasn't sure how to accept compliments.

That all eventually changed though. The same filthy pests that had haunted my nights in the chamber were not done with me yet. They wanted to remind me of their presence and the power they possessed over me. I had to make them sleep. All the vermin must sleep.

The spring of 1992 brought me back to where I had tried to escape from for so long. It brought me back to the chamber days. It occurred with the worst possible timing and exposed the vermin for who they really were.

As I sat waiting for our set design team to prepare the next scene in our follow-up production, *The Addams Family*, I decided to check my bag to see if I had any snacks left for the day. I opened my bag and quickly shoved my hand down to feel for any treats that might have settled at the bottom. While digging through the darkness, I felt something soft and hairy. I lifted my hand quickly. The other students around me, including Michael, sat with full attention. Without saying a word, I turned my bag over into the aisle, only to be met with a large faux rat dropping to the floor. In shock, I jolted onto the seat. Michael and the other students laughed as if the joke was intentional. I quickly became enraged at the thought of Michael and my fellow club members having a laugh at the expense of my mental status. I stood up, kicked the rat, grabbed my bag, and exited the theater aisle immediately.

THE VERMIN SLEEP

As I was leaving, I heard Michael joke, "Where are you going, Rat Bag?" It was at that moment, I knew that my past had been dug up and brought back from the dead. I knew there would be no end to this here. No peace until there were no vermin.

The following days were blurry as I made my way down the halls to the muffled giggles and laughs of the other students. Some of them made no noise when I passed. This was confirmation they too knew of the horrors that awaited them after the final bell. Though the incident was days removed, I was still furious that Michael and the other students had decided to go as far as place the fake rat into my bag. In every passing and grit of my teeth, I couldn't quell the increasing rage I felt towards Michael and the others.

I waited after our theater club met and asked Michael to stick around to help me with a few pieces of the set that were to be finished.

"Hey Alex, what do you need help with?"

Motioning for Michael to come behind the curtain and ask him to help me lift one of the background settings, I moved quickly and placed myself behind the curtain, waiting for him to continue towards the back. I reached for my hammer. As he came around the curtain, I lifted the yellow hammer back. It slipped, falling to the ground as Michael came around the corner.

"I thought you needed help to lift the set piece, not driving nails." He laughed and continued towards the back of the stage.

As if by divine intervention, our theater teacher followed closely behind him.

My palms sweating with anticipation, I decided to not move forward with my plans to bludgeon Michael, claw outward, in the skull. Helping the teacher and Michael stand the stage set on its braces, I still felt an unsatisfied sense of anger. He would live to scurry among the others for the remainder of his senior year.

CHAPTER SIX

Graduation came quickly with no additional discussion about my past. Michael had graduated and moved away to college. I was preparing for college and working a dead-end job at a local eatery, prepping meals and washing dishes. The owner of the restaurant was a loud and ill-tempered man by the name of Alfonso Diobrella. His ratio for accepting poor service and quick turnaround of dishes was an even split. I treated approaching him with the same manner that I treated the Old Bastard. Don't talk. Just listen. It seemed to garner favor with Alfonso as he treated me better than any of the other kitchen staff and took me under his wing.

In his kitchen, I quickly became the go-to representative when it came to moving orders quickly and without complaint. Alfonso would begin to teach me that the rats are not always visible. He had a love for gambling that would occasionally cause him to catch a visit by the local sharks. Like a rat to cheese. Always vigilant, though, he would get wind of their arrival and slip out the back door. It was almost instinctual for him. Almost like he could smell them coming and slip out right when they were walking in. It was as if he saw the trap and diverted before they could bring the hammer down.

One afternoon as I was arriving at the restaurant, Alfonso was out back, damp from profuse sweating. It looked like the dishwasher had turned on him and left.

"Al, come over here. I need you to take care of something for me. There's been an accident and I need you to do me a favor."

I kept with the practice of listening and not talking, as it had served me well up to this point.

"A guy came here looking for some money I owed, we got into a bit of a scuffle and well...he's in the trunk of my car."

I didn't move. I didn't know what to say. He took me over to the car, popped the trunk, and confirmed everything he had told me. There in the trunk, covered under a painter's tarp, was the deceased body of a slim man. His head looked to have been split with a blunt object. The blood slightly trickling from the open wound.

"Take the car, Al. Take it over near the edge of one of the lakes and burn it." This was the first time I saw a victim of blunt force trauma, but it would certainly not be the last.

I hesitated and Alfonso pleaded as if his life had depended on it, because it did. I eventually agreed, on the basis that once it was done, Alfonso would cease gambling. We both knew his promise was untrustworthy as the urge for him to roll dice or tap tables was too great.

I grabbed the keys and away I went, taking the can of gas Alfonso had supplied with me. His instructions were clear: Take the car the farthest away from the city skyline, set it ablaze, and find a payphone to ring him at the shop and he would send another co-worker to pick me up. He knew that eventually the shark's friends would come looking for him at the last place he ventured for a collection. Once again, like the rat he was, he was able to convince the shark's friends the shark had mentioned taking a generous sum of money to some casino down south in an attempt to double it.

THE VERMIN SLEEP

I parked the car and set it ablaze, miles from the city skyline. I made sure to open the trunk and pour the gasoline all over the corpse, making a mental note of what a dead body really looked like. I wandered for what must have been a few miles before coming to a local gas station with a payphone near the road.

I rang Alfonso's, expecting him to answer and send someone. I was wrong. After diverting the shark's friends in the other direction, Alfonso had quickly closed shop, gathered his money and what he could carry, and left immediately. The rat left me stranded at a gas station in the middle of nowhere. I only learned this after hitchhiking my way back into the city and arriving to see one of my other co-workers locking up the shop. He told me that Alfonso had left in a hurry and told my co-workers they were going to have to start looking for another job. He paid them all and told my co-worker to leave the keys in the mailbox.

I stood t in silence. Angry that someone I had trusted made me an accomplice to murder, and left me to hang for the crimes he had committed. I stood clinching my fists till the point that blood was ready to pour from my palms. My teeth were gritted to the point I could feel my gums give to the anger.

I realized though that the shark's buddies would come back sooner rather than later, looking for him. He had previously given them my name as a point of contact. Also, I overheard he had bought himself time, as the sharks only knew of Alfonso by the address of his restaurant and not by his home address within the city. Given that he had closed up shop only hours ago, he most likely figured he had several days to plan a solid getaway, or just lie low.

28

I would be damned if I would be sought after for the crimes of a rat named Alfonso Diobrella. I quickly went up the street to the late-night diner, grabbed a napkin, and scribbled down Alfonso's home address. I returned to the storefront and placed the napkin inside the rusty old mailbox that hung near the door.

Goodnight Alfonso, you rat bastard. Sleep well.

THE VERMIN SLEEP

CHAPTER SEVEN

I never heard from Alfonso again after that day. I made the decision to continue seeking employment on the opposite side of the city. I applied and was hired on a construction site for a brief time as I started scouring stagehand job listings via newspaper ads. This allowed me to hone my skills with my trusty hammer. I had managed to keep hold of my same Stanley hammer I had in high school. It was taken from the theater club when I graduated and was kept close ever since.

It had served me well and continued to do so as I worked on various locations within the city. It was during my times serving under the construction foreman that I became aware of something so vile I would soon learn the extent of my internal rage.

During a conversation between the foreman and a fellow carpenter, I heard discussion of some pictures that had been circulating. I paid it no attention when I first overheard the two talking and continued on with building a frame for a new home right outside the city limits. I was in deep focus when one of the crew yelled for me, motioning to come over to them.

As I walked over, I noticed a photograph in the hand of the crew member.

"Hey Alex, how old ya think?"

I gasped and stepped back. "What the fuck are you doing?" were the only words that could escape my mouth.

In his hands, he held two Polaroid pictures displaying what looked to be a young girl being assaulted. I could feel my blood begin to boil and my stomach turn to knots. I could sense the years of repressed rage and emotional torment were coming to the surface. Every blood vessel in my body felt like it had begun to constrict, and the memories of my own past flooded my brain.

"Alex, don't worry man! I don't know who she is but if you want to see some more just let me know. I got a guy uptown that can get you what you want."

It was at that very moment that I had committed to burying the bastard that was doing this. Another child. A child like myself. No more restraint.

I mentioned to the crew member that if he could get me a few more tonight then I'd pay him some big money.

He assured me he could make it happen and would have them for me tomorrow. "I knew you were a weird fuck, Alex. To quiet not to be."

I would soon discover I was more than a "weird fuck". He would soon discover this as well.

As the end of the day wrapped up, I waited in my car for the crew member to gather his items and make his way out to his own car. I wouldn't let this one go. I couldn't.

I drove behind him at a distance so as not to draw attention to myself. I noticed him pull into a small gas station just before entering the city, parking close to a payphone. He picked up the phone, deposited the money, and dialed. I watched from down the street, sweating from the anxiety and the rage. No matter; only one emotion would see its way through to the end of the evening.

THE VERMIN SLEEP

As he drove off I continued to follow, moving northward and into the area of Rogers Park. I watched as he went inside a well-kept home. I waited patiently. I waited with intent.

While waiting, I made notes of the location on the back of an old phone bill. I wrote with such force that the pen poked several tiny holes through the paper.

Eventually, after around thirty minutes, the crew member stepped outside and into his car down the street. I pursued him for a long while till we came to a stopping point. A two-story brick home that featured a screened front porch. Beautiful neighborhood for such an ugly pest.

I waited till he entered his home, watching for the lights to come on as he moved from room to room. I made a mental note earlier that he wore no wedding ring. No attachments to get in the way. Good.

I proceeded to put my worn leather work gloves on and gripped the hammer in my right hand. I made my way towards the side of the house and observed the rat sitting in his easy chair, eating what looked to be a microwave meal. The thoughts of home came flooding back. A vision of the Old Bastard bringing the meals to the sliding chamber door. It was time for the vermin to sleep.

I walked to the front of the house and knocked on the door. The porch light came on.

"Hello? Who's there?" He shuffled his feet as he walked to the door. "Alex! You weirdo! How'd you know where I live? Anyhow, come on in. I got those photos you wanted!'

I entered the darkened front porch, stepping directly behind the rat.

As he turned to grab the door handle to open into his living room, I lifted the hammer.

At that moment, the world froze, going silent, and time stood completely still. It suddenly became clear to me this being – this beast – had no soul. He was no longer fit for this world.

I brought the hammer down with the force to drive a nine-inch nail through a board. The sound of the hammer cracking through the rear of his skull coupled with the thud of impacting whatever shit-for-brains he had brought back memories. Memories of rats meeting the heels of my feet. The splatter was not what I had imagined. Small shards of skull and brain had fragmented to be left resting on my distressed work shirt.

He stood there briefly making mumbling noises, still trying to open the door, only to fall inside the doorway after his corpse forced it open. I quickly lifted him in the rest of the way. His body was much heavier than I had anticipated and called for dragging more than lifting. The adrenaline rushing through my veins pushed me to remove him from possible view of others. Once inside, I noticed he was still twitching. His eyes scanning the room with a hollow look behind them. I grabbed a nearby blanket, laid it over him, and proceeded to smash the remaining life from his head.

As I surveyed the area, I noticed the horrible pictures resting on the table beside his recliner. I grabbed the pictures and laid them across his carcass. I knew no one was going to come looking anytime soon, but I had no intention of staying. I grabbed my hammer and calmly made my way back to my truck. I looked into the rearview mirror and cleared any smattering of blood from my face, wiping it on my jeans. As I shifted in my seat, a few small fragments of bone fell to the floorboard.

THE VERMIN SLEEP

While driving off, a new sense of being came over me. It was the same sense of relief I felt in the chamber after dealing with the rodent infestation. I immediately went home and slept through the night. A beautiful sleep. And the vermin were sleeping too.

To my surprise, the next few days went smoothly. No one made any mention of where our fellow crew member might be. Several others made jokes that he was probably on a bender and suffering the worst hangover of his life.

I smirked and continued driving each nail with the same dedication and force I had used on the fool's skull. The drones were oblivious to anything and everything. I remember being comforted knowing there were no worries in regard to his well-being, and that I could continue to fly undetected for as long as I needed. This comfort allowed me to return to the address of the rat's nest where the horrid photographs were produced.

In the evenings, I would take post down the street and watch as rodent after rodent made their way into the house and scurry back out. Every one of them had to go and I had to make sure of it. I couldn't allow any other innocent beings to be tormented in chambers and forced to demonstrate perverse acts for these beasts. I knew all too well of the consequences that would follow them for the rest of their lives. There would be blood spilt and I was perfectly fine with making the cold concrete my canvas.

CHAPTER EIGHT

The following evenings, I sat in my aging pickup truck and watched. I began to make notes of who would show up to the den and how long they would stay. As I continued to watch, I also began to make plans for the next rodent that ran from the nest. This one appeared to be a middle -aged, unkempt, and overweight man. He walked with a cane to prevent him from tumbling due to what looked like a knee issue. The knee brace across his right knee appeared to slightly bulge as he walked along.

After watching the man return night in and night out, I could hold back the urge no longer. I decided to follow the portly pervert from the den to his home. He traveled west and slightly out of the city to a darkened street where he parked his car.

As I stepped out of my truck and onto the street, I could feel the anxiety give way to the rage. He started up his walkway and onto his small stoop, slowly unlocking and opening his door. When he began to enter into his home, I rushed behind him, forcing him to trip on his cane and hit the ground.

On top of him, I looked directly in his face and smiled, saying nothing as I lifted the hammer. His eyes bulged from his skull as the blunt side of the hammer met his forehead. He gurgled and attempted to plead for his life. It was of no use. Another wasted breath. The claw side made quick work of any noises attempting to leave his mouth. Blood began to quickly pool beside his fractured skull. The remains of his brains began to make their way towards the floor like a pile of sludge.

I stood back and glanced at the ground. The rat had been carrying the pictures, which now lay scattered around his corpse. I stepped backwards out the door, looking around to ensure that no one had been disturbed by my actions. Nothing. No one. I calmly walked back to the truck, started the engine, and casually drove home.

As I pulled into my parking spot at the apartment, my neighbor was taking his trash out. "Hey Alex! You mind giving me a hand tomorrow? I've got this table leg that's causing my table to be off balance."

While looking at my reflection in the large glass doorway, I noticed a smattering of blood had landed just below my right eye. Immediately, the fear of being caught and not being able to save others from the beasts crashed into me. The pulsing of blood and the feeling of dread must have been visible, but I had to maintain my composure.

"Sure, Steve." I continued on through the door hoping the dimly lit area had not given away my earlier actions.

Steve was from an older generation. Having served during the Vietnam War, his senses had been dulled by the atrocities he witnessed. Surely, he had not given the blood on my face a second look. Continuing into the apartment, I quickly moved to open my door.

"Been doing some painting Alex?"

He *had* noticed.

"Sure have, Steve. We're working on a high-rise downtown and the handrails weren't colored correctly. It's a building code issue."

He laughed, shook his head, and continued into his apartment.

I hurried to the bathroom, stripped my clothes, making sure to scrub every inch at least twice. Although another rat was sleeping, there was still so much more work to do.

The following day at work I made the decision to quit. The anxiety from the possibility of being caught had become too much. The foreman seemed upset that I was leaving. "It's a damn shame that we can't keep ya. Can't keep anyone around here anymore with half a brain."

I chuckled and calmly walked to my pickup. It was time to get rid of the den entirely and I knew that most of my time in the coming days would be used to surveil the rat's nest. I would make sure to park in separate locations throughout the week, making notes of how often the rats would come and go. The pattern became more defined after a few days. Usually between the hours of two and five o'clock, the action would slow to nothing. What was happening in there at that time? Why all of a sudden would there cease to be any movement? I knew that extermination during the day would be risky, but the opportunities were few, given the amount of traffic that frequented the nest. It had to be done though.

I began monitoring and observing the neighbors next. They were much more difficult to track and could have been rats themselves.

After nearly a week's worth of hours, I made the decision to enter the nest and make quick work of the owner.

I slowly exited my truck, making sure to conceal the trusty hammer that had served me so well up to this point. Walking to the porch, I could feel my adrenaline pumping. My nerves filled me to the busting point. There was no turning back. This was the point of no return for either myself or whatever was behind the front door.

THE VERMIN SLEEP

I stepped onto the enclosed porch and immediately noticed the smell of what I figured was rotting garbage. I decided to tuck my hammer into the back of my pants, so as not to raise any immediate alarms when the door opened. Knocking on the door, I could hear what sounded like a female scream, "I thought I told you assholes! I don't have any more copies of the photos!"

The door opened to a slim and leathery woman standing with a cigarette in her hand. "Who the fuck are you?"

I stood in silence for a moment, still processing what I was witnessing. I had dealt with plenty of male rats, but a female rat was not in the plans. I quickly decided to try to convince her I was sent by a friend. Thinking of a name and hoping it would stick, I quickly blurted out that a friend named Michael had sent me over for some new shots.

"Mikey?" I could tell that she was confused. "I just gave that asshole some new shots the other day! If he's not careful, there's gonna be about a dozen of Chicago's finest standing in my living room."

I continued to stand in the doorway, not making a decibel of noise.

"Fine, come in! You tell Mikey though that if I don't get my money for these shots, I'm cutting him out of the deal!"

I calmly stepped into the doorway.

"Wait right here. I've gotta run down stairs and get a few more shots."

The rage began to build. Every millisecond spent in the home drew a nearly uncontrollable need for extermination. This was the nest, and I was deep in the center. The woman went to a table on the other end of the room. Picking up a Polaroid camera, she disposed of

38

her cigarette in the ashtray situated on the table. "Damn thing needs more film! This stuff ain't cheap ya know!"

I slowly placed my hand behind my back, grabbing the hammer handle. Approaching the woman, she continued to pay me no attention. I slowly pulled the hammer out from behind and raised it, claw side facing her head. It was at that moment that she turned slightly away.

She stared at me with a horrified look as the claw came down, glancing the left side of her head and settling on her shoulder. I had missed my mark.

As she stumbled from the glancing blow and holding her now injured shoulder, I turned to the blunt side and swung like a baseball player towards her jaw. She hit the ground with a pleading look in her eyes.

I felt no remorse for her.

Unable to speak through her busted jaw, she raised her hands as the hammer fell its final blow. Her skull split like an egg, oozing out her decimated brain, which now resembled old chewing gum. Her body twitched lightly as the synapsis continued to signal the pain. She gasped and twitched for a few moments, then ceased.

I stepped back and a calm crept over me. No more rats in this nest. They will surely scatter. They will surely hide.

Unlike previous visits, I knew I had time to search the area. Time to make sure no others were in the house.

As I went to the upstairs area, I was stopped dead in my tracks. There was a child's room that looked like it was dressed for a young girl. I pushed the door open the rest of the way and peered inside. There was nobody in the room and nothing to suggest anyone had been harmed there. My mind quickly changed direction and I could see my own childhood room. The room before the chamber and the rats. It validated everything I was doing to rid the world of these beasts. If it gave a child a sense of normalcy, then it was all worth it.

Something felt completely off though as I continued searching around upstairs.

After spending a short amount of time checking the upstairs for any additional rats, I moved back down to the main floor. Continuing to look around, I heard a shuffling below my feet. The sound of metal on concrete.

As a moth to the flame, I began searching and opening every door in the house I could. I finally found one that opened to a stairwell into the darkness. I could hear sounds coming from the cellar. Reaching for the light switch on the side, I heard a call ring out from the darkness.

"Momma? Is that you?"

My knees nearly buckled. I had to keep it together as I knew I was not ready for what I was going to find. I slowly opened the door and proceeded down the stairs. A dim light illuminated a corner of the cellar. On the wall, a chain was attached and, on that chain, a small and defenseless child. Bound by a collar that had worn marks around her neck.

As I started towards her, I could see her eyes expand in that look of impending harm.

Reaching to grab the collar and release her, she started to scream a horrible scream. I quickly covered her mouth, explaining that she didn't need to worry anymore. Removing the collar, she stood in shock.

"No one will hurt you anymore. Understand?"

She nodded.

"You're going to stay down here for ten minutes after I go upstairs, then you're going to call the police. Do you understand me?"

Once again, she nodded. Her body had been ravaged by rats and the stench of the basement summoned memories I thought were dead and buried.

I quickly moved back up the basement, reassuring her that everything was going to be alright. She didn't move the entire time I was near. A ghost of a child that once was but was no more.

I rushed to my truck down the street. I sat there for a few minutes. Far down the street the appearance of flashing red and blue lights signaled that it was time for me to make my exit. The police would soon be swarming the area and anyone within then blocks would be stopped and interrogated. I gently pulled off and out of sight of any potential police situations.

As I drove off and onto the side streets far from the home, the knots in my stomach began to tighten. I knew the little girl would see the horrors inside the home. I knew she had gotten a good look at me. The horrors she experienced in that basement most likely trumped what she was going to walk in on upstairs. She might actually be able to sleep through the night without rats crawling over her.

THE VERMIN SLEEP

CHAPTER NINE

I arrived home late. Much later than I had intended. The whole ordeal of extermination had taken its toll on me. I immediately jumped into the shower and scrubbed away any spots of blood that their way to my face. As the blood slowly drained into the tub, I still did not have the feeling of relief I sought. I knew there were more vermin that needed to be exterminated. I had only cleared one of the dens. How many more were there? Where were they? I continued to question as I scrubbed my hair violently. More beasts meant there was more work to do.

I couldn't sleep that night. Lying in bed and thinking about the atrocities I had seen in the basement, I decided to give way to the morning.

After starting my coffee, I turned on my television and quickly made sure to adjust the loose antennas. I finally settled on a local channel broadcasting the news.

I almost spilled my coffee when the anchor began giving the details of my latest late-night visit.

"The Chicago Police Department are currently investigating a murder and a child pornography ring in the northern neighborhood. After receiving a distressed phone call from a young girl, police discovered the deceased mother of the child inside the home. Further details are still being gathered. We'll have more on this horrific crime scene, tomorrow."

They knew and they were quickly piecing the clues together.

I decided I would continue to rid the world of vermin, regardless of police involvement. They had done nothing for the little girl in the basement. It was me who had saved her from the brutality and prevented any additional problems for other children. If I hadn't been there, she wouldn't be free. I wasn't done.

The following day I took a trip to a truck stop just outside the city. I knew they would have exactly what I needed to continue to rid the world of the disgusting and vile vermin. I made my way to the aisle that contained the maps. Grabbing two maps of the city, I moved to the counter where a young man was working.

"I can tell you where not to go to if you need."

I asked the cashier to describe the areas he was most familiar with being unsafe.

He pointed out several areas on the map that he had heard stories about, where death and kidnappings were a regular occurrence. I mentioned I had my young son with me and wanted to make sure I stayed clear of anywhere that could cause him harm.

"Ah, I would definitely steer clear of this area then. Lots of kiddie-diddlers there."

I quickly asked the cashier if I could borrow a pen and began making notes of the places he suggested I not visit.

I paid and thanked the cashier for being so helpful. He had given me everything I needed to know where to look next.

Arriving back at my apartment building, I hurried up the stairs and inside. Opening the map, I placed it across the table and began examining the neighborhoods the cashier had warned me to avoid.

After picking my next location, I rang up the local police precinct in those neighborhoods. Introducing myself as a single father who is expecting to move into the area, I asked the answering officer if there were any known registered sex offenders in the area. Typically, without as much as a breath, they would divulge the names and addresses of the bastards and recommend another adjoining neighborhood to consider. I assured them I would with a passive-aggressive response before ending the call. As soon as the receiver was down, I would start placing indicating markers of all the known pedophiles in that neighborhood. Eventually, the map was littered with tiny black dots as though a rodent had crawled across the map and shit all across the city of Chicago.

After plotting out the next nests that needed clearing, I decided it was time for some fresh air. Walking into the local mini-mart, I noticed the headline on a local paper: Vigilante. Killer. Certainly, I was a vigilante, but a killer? The term used was stretched across the front page in an attempt to present me as an evil monster. I am far from that. I was merely getting rid of all the unneeded vermin running through our streets and invading our homes.

The paper described details of victims being found in a pool of blood with their skulls showing signs of blunt force trauma. The paper failed to detail anything about the horrendous crimes these assholes had committed. They simply labeled them as pedophiles. That was an understatement. These were not merely pedophiles; they were the monsters who climb out from under beds when they left their children's room at night. They were the undertow that pulls their children under on a sunny day at the beach. These fucking monsters. The paper vilified me and touted the monsters as victims. This could happen no more. *The Tribune* would soon understand what I was doing and why I was doing it.

CHAPTER TEN

That night I picked a location on the west side of Chicago. A small neighborhood called Brookfield. This was where the police had given up the name of a Joseph Belton. I made plans to visit the neighborhood the next day and scout out the address. The drive was some distance from my apartment building, so I would need to get some gas before heading over that direction. The cost of gas had risen to nearly ninety-five cents, and I wasn't sure of my available cash.

After looking at my wallet, realizing it had been weeks since I last worked, and the money was drying up, I decided to stay home and scour the classifieds, hopeful the next opportunity to tune my instrument would present itself. While searching, the most glorious opportunity shown itself to me. There was a position for a local cable access children's show, *Lucy's Playground*, which needed a maintenance man and set builder. I quickly cut the listing from the paper and stuck it on the fridge.

The visions of my youth and the late nights watching my favorite children's shows suddenly flooded my mind. I was taken back to a time of sitting with my mother and excitedly explaining to her my favorite characters' backstories. Damn it! I cannot go back there. I cannot rewind or catch a rerun of those days. The present is the true horror of living.

Immediately the next morning I went to the phone and rang the number on the job posting. A kind elderly lady answered, and we spoke about my history in construction, my love for children's shows like *Lucy's Playground* and the possibility of being a part of the show. I could tell my enthusiasm caught her off guard.

"You're not one of those weirdo kid chasers, are you?"

I quickly assured her that I was the exact opposite of that, and she had zero worries.

She laughed. I laughed.

Offering me a chance to interview, I thanked the lady and told her I would see her on Friday.

After hanging up the phone, I could feel the joy rush over me. The dreams of my youth were finally coming to fruition. Everything I had wanted as a child was possible. In a haze of adrenaline, I hopped into my car and drove to Brookfield. There was work to be done and I knew my opportunities to scout the neighborhood were going to be few and far between once I started the new job.

Waiting in my car, I watched the door to Joseph Belton's apartment. For what must have been a few hours, I sat quietly, propping the newspaper up to the wheel, and then back down to ensure I didn't miss the door opening out of my peripheral. Suddenly, without any excitement, the door opened. Out stepped a thin-stretched man with short hair and a smooth face. His appearance didn't fit the grotesque features of the previous victims.

I continued watching as he sat on the second story walkway of the apartment building. The doors were too close together to exterminate him at the apartment. *The neighbors might hear him hit the ground or scream.* This would need a different approach. I sat, watched, and waited some more.

47

THE VERMIN SLEEP

After leaving to grab a quick bite and returning to the apartment complex that evening, I noted that the lights were off. It appeared Joseph was no longer home. This signaled several possibilities. Regardless, I decided to wait no matter how long it took. This one could not get away. His sexual assault charges were too heavy.

After about an hour, he arrived back to the apartment complex. I quickly made a mental note of the car that he was driving: a small red hatchback sedan. A very distinct car and easy to spot among the others. I hesitated, wondering if I should return another night.

He began grabbing items from the rear of the car. Several bags of groceries that carried weight. I knew it was time. His hands were full. Mine, empty. His focus was on his apartment. Mine, on him. The streetlights were the only illumination for the area, and before he hit the sidewalk, it would be lights out for another vermin.

As he continued to grab bags out of his car, I swung open the car door and began to slowly walk towards him. He was focused at first, but the sound of my footsteps creeping up on him caught his attention. He looked up and smiled. It was at this moment I could smell the odor of his victims coming off his breath. His smile spoke volumes about whom he really was – a rodent.

As he smiled, I began to raise the hammer. His smile quickly turned to horror and I could sense the contents of his stomach making their way to his throat. Bringing the hammer down, claw-side facing his skull, the cracking sounded like walnuts being smashed under pressure. His left eye immediately left the socket as he crashed to the ground, dropping all the grocery bags and bringing the hammer with him, still lodged into his oozing open skull.

I applied a strong hold on the hammer, ripping it away and carrying pieces of bone and brain with it. When I stepped back, I felt the once glaring eye squish beneath the heel of my foot, nearly causing me to slip.

I stood there, staring at my work for what felt like eternity. The comfort it brought beckoned back to leaving the chamber. I turned to go, hearing neighbors open their apartment doors, covered my face with my sleeve, and retreated.

Another night and another good rest.

CHAPTER ELEVEN

Friday finally arrived and I awoke early, filled with excitement at the possibility of getting the job of my dreams. I spent that morning making sure I prepared myself to show the potential employers my capabilities as an expert in carpentry.

I also made sure to run through practice swings, imagining the villains at the other end of my tool.

I arrived fifteen minutes early and waited to be called back. The elderly lady I had spoken to on the phone seemed just as excited as I was to get the interview. She kept herself positioned so that her eyes and permed brilliant white hair were just barely visible over the front counter. Her smile told stories that would assure even the most hardened individuals that everything was going to be alright. In a certain light, she reminded me of my mother. Sincere. Genuine. Comforting. I knew immediately we would be getting along quite well if I received employment.

"Alex, Mr. Sullivan would like to speak with you now."

I stood up and made my way to a back office where sat the show's primary director, Frank Sullivan. He was a short and portly individual with dark black hair and a mustache that would give Tom Selleck a run for his money. He appeared in good spirits as I sat down slowly.

"Mr. Felmer, it looks like you have a lot of experience throwing a hammer around, but what do you know about television?"

I explained to him that growing up I was always infatuated with the sets of children's shows and how they were constructed. I informed him this infatuation turned into a career as I had worked construction, and now an opportunity to marry both my construction skills and love for children's show growing up was a dream come true. His smile continued to widen as I spoke. He loved everything he heard.

"Well, it definitely looks like we've got a perfect match!"

I held back the joy, thanking Mr. Sullivan. We arranged the start date within the next week. Perfect – it would allow me to scout my next location and get one more extermination before starting my job.

The following few days were spent scouting. After studying the map, I chose an area I had been familiar within my youth. My next target lived in a small brick home near the Chicago Zoo. Easy for me to find and navigate the area.

For what must have been less than twenty-four hours, I had my next problem sorted out. This rat was younger than the previous vermin. Michael Stephens, compared to previous predators, looked to be in good physical condition. I watched the homestead that Friday evening and decided I would make my presence known the following day.

I decided to drive back home in the most amazing state of mind. I had landed the job of my dreams and here I was with another potential vermin to destroy. The timing was incredible. It finally felt like the world was balancing for me. As if some being above or below had decided to grant me a well full of luck. A well, that I would soon find, had run dry.

THE VERMIN SLEEP

That Saturday morning, I made sure the neighbors were nowhere to be found. Exiting my car, I tucked my trusty yellow hammer behind my belt and made my way to young Michael's home. As I approached the door, I could hear the loud sound of the television in the living room, indicating he was home and my job would be unheard of by the neighbors. I knocked and waited.

"Who is it?!"

I yelled back that I was with the local cable company and needed to check on replacing his television connection.

He quickly flung open the door and offered me entrance, closing the door behind me. As quickly as he had turned around, I grabbed my hammer. Suddenly, he was face to face with me. He had seen me raise the hammer up over his head and now there was a struggle. This was all new to me. The others had gone so quietly.

I brought the hammer down, grazing his arm with the blunt side and leaving an immediate bruise with a slight cut. I had hit him with enough force to bring down the largest bull, but the blow didn't faze him.

He immediately ran towards the backdoor of his home, screaming for help. As quickly as it had started, it was over. He knew my face. He knew my intentions. The rat had seen the trap and was quick to escape.

I grabbed the door handle and quickly made my way from the home, tucking the hammer so that it was hidden from sight. Hopping into my truck down the street, I proceeded to leave, using the quickest route I knew out of the area. As I was leaving, the neighbors began poking their heads out of their doorways, scanning for the source of the horrified screams.

That night, I turned on the news to see if there was any mention of the incident. Of course, the news media had once again glanced over the fact that the "victim" was a child predator. They chose to showcase me as the madman who was hell-bent on murder. If only they knew that the horrifying truth. It was about keeping the children safe from the bastards who would torture them. It was about preventing the rats from crawling into their homes and beds. This was of no importance to the media. I was a killer with a body count to report.

Michael Stephenson managed to give the police enough details for them to create a sketch to broadcast. A poorly drawn sketch, but a sketch nonetheless. I knew I would have to make adjustments to my appearance over the next week. This would distance my face from the sketch and allow things to grow cold for the police.

Luckily, Michael hadn't seen my vehicle, as he was too busy screaming for help from his backyard.

They know too much. Looks like I'll ride the public transit for a little while.

CHAPTER TWELVE

T hat Monday I made my way via bus to the studio front entrance. I was greeted by the security guard and provided him with my ID. As he glanced over my ID, I noticed his face turn to confusion.

"You look familiar. Do I know you from anywhere?"

Shit. He had probably seen the sketch on the news this weekend. I could feel my breakfast quickly turn upside down in my stomach. Did he know or just making a lucky guess?

I assured him we had never met and that I was actually new to the area.

He quickly laughed and shrugged.

I told him I'm sure we'll be seeing more of each other, and he waved me on into the gated entrance. I had never felt so much relief in my life.

I continued to the building where the stage for the children's show was set. As I entered the building, the elderly lady I had talked to previously waved and smiled the biggest and most comforting smile I had seen in so long.

"My name is Stacey. If you ever need anything, please come find me and I'll get you whatever you need."

I thanked her and proceeded through towards the stage area.

It was like something out of a dream. A dream that I had imagined being part of since I was five years old. The stage area was a wide open, hanger-like room with only a few built walls off to the side. The cameras and sound equipment filled the void between the entrance and the stage area. *If this is heaven, then I surely have done the world a great service in my life.* The lights hanging from the ceiling illuminated the stage where a living room setting had been assembled.

I stared for a while, taking in the sights, sounds, and smells of what was once only a dream. The sound of production assistants busily working to get everything ready for the next shoot grabbed my attention. It was as if they were worker ants, moving individually but collectively like some sort of hive mind. I imagine I stuck out like a sore thumb standing there with my overalls and toolbox to my side, gawking at all the different Activity. I was awe-struck for the first time in my life. It was bliss.

"Alex! You made it! We're so glad to have you here!" The director, Frank Sullivan, greeted me with open arms and began showing me all the different areas of the set. His ability to describe the inner workings of each team member brought to life why he was the director.

"Alex, this is your area back here."

We walked to a small woodshop in the far back corner of the building. I'm sure my eyes, wide as spotlights, spoke volumes about my excitement. Every tool an avid carpenter could want was right before my eyes. Frank knew immediately that I was impressed.

"Well, looks like these keys belong to you. One goes to the building entrances, and the others are for your shop and its lockers."

When he dropped the keys into my hand, I felt a calming sensation I had only felt from my previous encounters with the deadbeats.

"We'll go over the shoot schedule later today and make sure to get you the badge, so you don't have to deal with the security guard out front. He can be nosy and a bother when you're in a hurry."

Thanking the director, I went to work checking out every tool and making sure my favorite hammer had a new place to call home. A place to sleep without any vermin finding it.

It was later that day the director called everyone in for an introduction and gave details regarding the upcoming season's shoots.

"Everyone, please welcome the newest edition to our crew, Alex Felmer! He'll be working to make sure that our sets are kept in top shape and also hammering away at a few new pieces we'll be adding this season. Be nice, he carries a hammer around." He laughed. They laughed. I smiled.

I was welcomed by the crew with open arms. For the first time since high school, I felt like I finally had a place. Though I was hesitant, I still felt this would be my permanent place of employment.

The rest of the afternoon was filled with stories from the crew about their experiences with previous set builders and dodging faulty pieces that weren't constructed properly. I assured them they had nothing to worry about, as I knew my way around a hammer. It was comfortable – too comfortable – but I had the job of my childhood dreams and everyone seemed so nice.

Almost, too nice.

CHAPTER THIRTEEN

Over the next few weeks, I spent every available hour I could in the woodshop. I would get the blueprints from the set designer and go to work creating the sets and making sure the rest of the builds were properly maintained. I must have hammered every nail and cut every piece of wood that they had.

Mr. Sullivan was extremely impressed and would occasionally stop by to see if everything was going well and if I needed anything. He accommodated every request, though they were exceedingly rare. The production assistants brought me coffee on an almost daily routine and made sure to let me know when catering had arrived. How could anyone want to leave this job? I was not bothered with others' work and could focus on mine alone.

It was a Wednesday afternoon during my fifth month of employment when the production assistant came around to the woodshop. "Hey Alex, Mr. Sullivan is calling an all-hands-on-deck meeting tomorrow morning. The cast for the next season will be arriving and they want everyone to get acquainted with them. It helps everyone to know everyone in case there are any questions. Sound good?"

I nodded and the assistant went on her way, making the rounds to inform all other team members.

Later that night, I made a decision to let the media frenzy surrounding my recent exploits cool down. The news stories would occasionally still come on the television, and the paper was still printing the sketch composite. I had begun dieting some and gradually reducing my facial hair, so as not to look too conspicuous. The changes were gradual and would hopefully deter any additional questions from nosy individuals. The change might have been doing me some good too. I was starting to feel more comfortable than ever. Though I would still get an itch to do surveillance runs through the rodent-infested neighborhoods, I chose to stay in and make an attempt at a normal life.

It was an attempt, at least.

The next day, I made sure to wear my best overalls and buttoned up shirt to the cast introduction. I had been given a badge, so I was allowed to walk right past the intrusive security guard, but not without the occasional glare. He knew something but could not figure out what. That was perfectly fine with me.

I would make it a point to arrive early every day to talk to Stacey. She made it a point to bring me cookies on a weekly basis. We had grown to become distant yet kindred spirits through our discussions and she gave me no trouble and only smiles. If only my mother could meet her. They would have been the best of friends.

I arrived before the cast, so I decided to clean every tool and piece of equipment. I wanted to make the best impression possible so the cast knew they had the best set builder anywhere. As the loudspeaker called an all-hands-on-deck meeting, I quickly made my way over to join the rest of the crew while the cast were led into the stage area. One by one, they introduced themselves. I followed along introducing myself and my position within the crew.

As the cast gave their introductions, I noticed the children were all very soft-spoken and quiet when they were not spoken to. I began to get that uneasy feeling that called back to the days of the Old Bastard's chamber. I had seen this before and knew all too well that something was wrong, but I was in no place to voice any concerns. If I had done so, then there would be questions, and someone might go digging to find out the truth about my past. I couldn't have that, so I decided to remain silent, but also vigilant. The smell of the rats on the chamber floor crept into my memory, and I knew if there were vermin present, they would not stay hidden for long.

The cast greeted us one by one, shaking our hands and introducing themselves alongside their parents. Most of the parents kept their focus on me. It was as if my silence was off-putting to them, and they needed more from me. I was giving them none of it. I was here to build the sets and that was all.

This started to draw questions though. Which one of these parents were actually the beast? Were they all beasts in disguise? Was it a cult for trafficking children through the entertainment business? So many questions flooded my mind and the sudden sense of dread overcame every thought passing through my mind.

As the cast moved on, Frank came to me and, leaning in, whispered that the parents felt uncomfortable with my presence and asked if I could spend most of the shooting time in the woodshop area.

I hesitated, laughed, and assured him I would do whatever was needed to keep the cast safe and happy.

He patted my back and thanked me.

It didn't feel right. None of it. As quickly as it felt comfortable, it felt uncomfortable.

THE VERMIN SLEEP

CHAPTER FOURTEEN

The next few days I stayed hidden from the cast as they went about their business shooting and relaxing in their trailers out back. All the while, watching the news and reading the paper to see if the police had gathered any new clues. Much to my surprise, the only information they were able to gather was that a blunt object had been used in all the attacks. That was all they needed to know, and as far as I was concerned, that was all there was to know.

In hindsight, I realize the teachings of the Old Bastard came in handy. I was able to keep my mouth shut and not discuss my utter hatred for all the beasts prowling the streets and homes of those innocent children. If only for a brief moment, I was enjoying the time away from the killing fields and starting to appreciate my own work in the shop. The time would be short-lived, though. The rats would eventually show themselves to me again.

It was a normal Tuesday afternoon when I was looking through a vending machine for a snack. I was approached by the show's star, Lucy. A curious, six-year-old, fragile little girl who had a world ahead of her and was almost oblivious to it. She was standing behind, holding a small stuffed parrot and waiting for me to finish.

"Which one is your favorite?"

I turned to see she was talking to me.

"Me? I like pecan rolls myself. My mom used to make them for me when I was a kid. Looks like I got a bit too hungry though and already ate all of them. I can't stop at just one, you know?"

She laughed, then I laughed. It was then that I noticed the small stuffed bird she was holding and asked if he had a name.

"Yep! His name is Sammy. I got him on vacation last year and now he goes everywhere with me!"

"Sammy, huh? That's a great name! I used to read a magazine called *Zoobooks*, and one of the covers was a bird that looked just like Sammy!" I immediately was drawn to Lucy's good nature. A curious and innocent child. Much like I was at one point.

Her eyes lit up. "I love animals! Do you have it still?"

I hesitated before telling her I believed I did. She grinned so large that half her face disappeared behind the smile.

"I'll tell you what, if I can find that magazine, I'll bring it in for you and Sammy to read."

I could tell she was ecstatic to hear that.

"My name's Lucy. What's yours?"

I told her my name was Alex and I built the sets.

"Well, I better get back to the stage. My parents are waiting and Mr. Sullivan always says it's impolite to keep people waiting. I really hope you can find that book, Mr. Alex. I really wanna read it!" She turned and ran back towards the stage area for the next shots.

That evening, I searched my closet for the back issues of the *Zoobooks* I had kept all these years. I couldn't part from them. They were the closest thing I had to remembering my mother. Remembering who she was and what mattered to her: my happiness. After searching for a brief time, I came across the issue about birds and placed it on the table near my door. I was going to make it a point to give Lucy the book and hopefully the parents

61

would be understanding. Hopefully, it would make Lucy just as happy as it had me when I received it.

The work that day had exhausted me, and I chose to retire to bed before I started getting that uneasy feeling. The itch that requires violent scratching to satisfy.

The following day, I grabbed the *Zoobook* and headed to work. As I passed Lucy's chair near the makeup area, I placed the *Zoobook* on the seat and proceeded to the woodshop. Several hours passed and I heard the shop door rattle and slam shut. It was Frank. His face spoke volumes about his anger.

"I thought I told you not to talk to the kids in the cast? The parents found that stupid book you left on Lucy's chair and now they are upset. One of the makeup artists saw you place it on the chair on your way in! Don't be an idiot, Alex! You got it good here and I would hate to have to let you go over something like this! Stay in your shop area and don't talk to the kids! Understood!?"

I quietly nodded.

He quickly turned and stormed out of the shop area and off into the stage area. It was clear the parents didn't understand the intent of my actions, yet I decided it best to leave things alone and continue with my work.

That evening upon arriving at home, I glanced over the map displaying the plague of rodents across Chicago. The urge to purge the city of more beasts was nearly overwhelming. I picked a small an upscale neighborhood that showed several indicators for activity.

As the urge to scout began to burn within, I reminded myself of the new job and how happy my mother would be for me. I was reminded of the Old Bastard as well, though. It was the equivalent of having good and evil rest on your shoulders while giving me directions. This time I chose to listen to the good. Maybe it was time for the rattraps to be handled by the police. Maybe it was time to retire my hammer as a killer and use it only on the sets.

CHAPTER FIFTEEN

O ver the course of the following weeks, I started to notice some unusual tendencies from the director. He paid more attention to Lucy than the other cast members. I would often overhear him asking her questions about her personal life. He would bring her gifts like candy and assorted toys, none of which the other kids would receive. Though no one else in the crew seemed to take notice, I became hyperaware of it. With that, her demeanor began to shift. She was becoming increasingly uncomfortable with the shoots.

Though I made an effort to stay away from the area, I would receive regular calls to tweak or adjust different portions of the stage. Some days, the other children would arrive much later than Lucy, and the rest of the cast was nowhere to be found. I found this unusual, but there were certain days when the rest of the cast were not needed for filming.

The day I saw Frank leave Lucy's trailer immediately brought my full attention to him. He hadn't seen me, but I clearly saw him. I was unloading some lumber that had just arrived in the backlot near all the cast's trailers. It wasn't unusual for a female production assistant to be in the trailers with the cast members, advising them on their upcoming shots and when to expect to be called to the stage, but not the director. Aside from Frank leaving the trailer, there seemed to be no parents following in tow. Something inside my gut began to churn and I decided that day to dive deeper into the matter.

When break was called, I made my way to the catering area near the vending machines, where I knew the cast would gather for snacks and to talk about their day. If there were any bastards present, I would root them out and deal with them as needed. Lucy approached the vending machines, glancing over all the other snacks that were available. I quickly moved towards the machine and knelt down in front of her. I could see the trouble in her eyes.

"Hey Lucy, how are you on this fine day?" I asked her, acting as if everything was fine.

"It's ok. I'm just a little tired today. Mr. Sullivan has been making me work a lot." Lucy was cautious in her wording.

I asked about Mr. Sullivan leaving her trailer, her response was that they were discussing the shots he wanted in the next few scenes, but her eyes told me a completely different story. They told me there was a rat in our presence.

"Lucy, you know you can tell one of us if you aren't feeling comfortable with something." I made sure she understood the concern in my voice.

"I know, Mr. Alex. It will be alright. My parents told me to follow any instructions that Mr. Sullivan gives me and to do as he says." Lucy muttered.

Every day after, I observed Frank as he went about his routine. I made mental notes of Lucy's whereabouts when he was not within sight. As time passed, I had the vermin's routine down so well I could recite it like a line in a show.

Then suddenly, he began to frequent Lucy's trailer. It became increasingly clear what was happening – and what *had* to happen. I couldn't let him continue to do the evil deeds he had done. I began making myself more present outside the studio area and closer to the trailers outside. The first few times he glanced around and made no notion he sensed anything was wrong. Then one day he cornered me.

"What are you doing out by the cast's trailers? I've seen you out there quite a bit and I don't think you need to be."

I could smell the fear dripping off him. He knew I was onto him. His sense of being would soon be diminished though. He would meet a wrath he had never known. I told him the break tables were located nearby, and I had chosen that spot to eat my lunch and take my breaks.

"Well, find a new place. The parents have told you and I've warned you. Take this as your final warning, Alex." The stench was overwhelming. He would require a special end. A truly grand finale.

That evening, I made preparations. I no longer would need the map, as the other rats were of no concern. This would be my greatest catch yet. I sat on my bed with polish and cleaned my hammer. I could see my reflection in the steel.

Soon, Mr. Frank Sullivan would catch a glimpse of himself in it as well. The last glimpse he would ever see. The rat bastard had to go.

CHAPTER SIXTEEN

Walking into work that morning, I was suddenly stopped by Stacey. She had a very discerning look on her face. "Alex. Someone called from the hospital downtown. They said it had something to do with your father? Is everything alright?"

At that moment, my mind started to spiral. I could see the chamber. I could smell the rats' entrails and blood rotting on the floor. It was as if the Old Bastard knew what was to come and chose to make one last appearance in my life to see me return to the chamber.

I stood there silently for a prolonged moment. No noise. Nothing.

"Alex, are you alright?"

I reassured her everything would be fine as she handed me a name and number on a piece of studio stationery. I smiled the worst smile possible and thanked her for relaying the message.

She knew better. She knew something was wrong. Her usual upbeat personality had turned into a stony appearance.

It was no use. I had business to attend to and couldn't be bothered by the Old Bastard.

I made my way to the woodshop and set my stuff on the bench. The production assistant stuck her head in the door. "Alex! We're gonna need you to stay a little later today to finish up some of the new set pieces."

THE VERMIN SLEEP

Good. I'm going to need a little extra time today. I've got big plans for my next showing and can't be bothered with time constraints.

I made my way to the stage area and readied my tools. As I began to unpack, I saw Frank Sullivan in the other area of the studio, prepping the cast for the day's shot. Glancing over, our eyes met for what would be one of the final times. I was certain of that as I smiled, gritting my teeth with immense pressure.

I continued about my regular preventative maintenance schedule. Making sure that every bolt, nut, and washer were securely fastened. I couldn't have any issues today. My mind was elsewhere.

After the midday takes, I was once again greeted by Lucy. She made an effort to talk to me and let me know things were alright, even when I knew damn well they weren't. She would stay just out of sight of Sullivan and her parents, so as not to cause any uproar. It made no difference to me. I could sense the problem was growing out of control and there was only one way to solve it.

After telling me all about her new stuffed animal tiger she had gotten from the production assistant, I calmly made my way back to the woodshop to prepare for the final act. I made sure my hammer was properly prepared and there was no damage to the handle. I covered the floors with vinyl mats so any mess left behind would be easily cleared. I already knew of the perfect place to dispose of a body thanks to my former employer. Mr. Sullivan would be taking a trip, and no one would be the wiser as the show's season was coming to an end. Sure, there were more seasons planned, but no director had yet been selected. I learned this from the production assistant just days before during a staff meeting.

Waiting for the final shoot to finish felt like eternity. Right before the last scene of the season, I motioned for the production assistant. I let them know that after everything was wrapped, I wanted to thank Mr. Sullivan for giving me the job and congratulate him on such excellent work. I knew the opportunity to inflate his ego would not be turned down. I made sure to emphasize there was no hurry because I was working late.

The assistant hurried back to the director's chair, whispered into his ear, and the biggest shit-eating grin came across his face. He looked over, smiling, and proceeded to give a strong thumbs-up. It had worked exactly as I knew it would. The rat had taken the cheese and now all that was left was to close the trap.

THE VERMIN SLEEP

CHAPTER SEVENTEEN

I sat till I could hear the sound of the stage lights turn off. Several of the cast thanked me with a blanket statement they offered the rest of the stage. It was no concern. I was used to the disingenuous nature of humanity. Oddly enough, there was no sign of Lucy or Frank. My blood boiled to the point my veins were pressure cookers. Then, as if a sign from above or below, the click of the door stopped. That was the indicator only a small few remained.

As I sat quietly waiting in the shop, I heard approaching footsteps echo beyond the door. I sat, patiently waiting for the opportunity to call for one last shot. One final bow. As the door slowly opened, I saw before me the very creature I sought to destroy: director Frank Sullivan. This was to be his final cut.

"Hey Alex! I really appreciate your hard work this season. I know things haven't always felt like they were the best between us, but I think you did a hell of a job keeping the sets in order. Trust me when I say that I'm certain the network will have you back for the next season."

I stood up, slowly and in a solid motion.

As if to provide some unspoken truce, he reached out for a handshake. I reached for my trusty hammer. A look of confusion crossed his face as I raised the shiny weapon above my head, my eyes fixated on a small section of his forehead.

I brought the hammer down to bash his frontal lobe rapidly, each time the hammer threw fragments of skull, brain, and blood. I didn't plan for a messy end, but it didn't matter much now.

His hand was still extended as blood poured from a massive open wound near his hairline, the tint of brownish pink showing through the open portion of his forehead. He had no idea what had just happened. His emotionless facial expression assured me of this. Standing there, swaying with his hand still outstretched. The nerves were not yet firing on all cylinders, or there weren't many left.

I slowly cleaned the remains from my hammer, exposing the shine that had been covered by fragments of skull and brain. Then, without any sound, he lowered his hand and stared into my eyes. I could smell the vermin's stench permeate the air around me. The smell of fear and the realization that all hope was lost.

It stinks of an awful odor.

Just like the others before, Mr. Sullivan collapsed to the ground in a twitching pile of shattered humanity. The type of twitch that tells you there is just enough life remaining for them to understand the horror of their end.

Watching the rat convulse brought me a sense of comfort. No matter how strange it sounded, the very thought of one last predator in the world created a sense of self-worth. I was meant for this, and he was meant to be here.

As he attempted to mutter a word, I proceeded to provide a reminder to only speak when spoken to by pressing a steel-toe boot into his mouth. His tongue forced to taste the filth on the sole. His squirming body was quickly silenced after that, apart from a few moans. He was losing blood and hope simultaneously. I was glad. The pain others had endured at his hands was going to last much longer than the pain of his death. At that moment, I could sense my mother patting me on the back and thanking me for doing away with the Old Bastards of the world. Making sure they couldn't bring any more pain to anyone else.

As I watched the life leave the beast's body, I began wrapping him in the tarp. I looked up to see the horrified expression on Stacey's face as she stood in the doorway. There was no exchange of words. Just a blank stare between us. She knew everything and at that moment the knots in my stomach began to turn. She stood there holding her hand over her mouth in a state of shock. She slowly backed around the corner and disappeared. I didn't know how to react. This was the first time someone had witnessed my work. I already knew what was to come.

I hurried to secure the body in the bloody tarp and make my way to the truck. There was no use in attempting to hide what had been done. I turned the engine over and away I went in the direction of the hospital.

I quickly pulled into the parking spot and went directly to the front desk. I could hear the sound of an ambulance leaving the bay with the sirens blaring. I already knew where they were heading. They didn't need to hurry though. It was too late for Frank Sullivan.

I asked the receptionist for my father's room and was told to talk to the chaplain. I was too late to make peace with the Old Bastard. To make peace with myself. I decided it was best to leave and wait for the inevitable elsewhere. I felt relief as I left the hospital, knowing I had done what I set out to do, and it was done right.

Driving back to my apartment, I knew it wouldn't be long till the police arrived. There was no use in putting up a fight. What was done was done.

It took them a mere two hours before they were beating on the apartment door. When the door flung open, I sat motionless on the couch. The memories of being rescued from the chamber were now replaced with being placed in handcuffs and led like a rat down to the waiting police car. The media caught wind of everything and were waiting outside. The bastards finally got their chance to see what they were so desperate to see. A beast being led to his chamber.

CHAPTER EIGHTEEN

I sat alone in my cell for several days before the chaplain came to deliver the news I already knew.

I had no words for him. No need to waste any more of the breath I would surely be robbed of eventually.

He described the Old Bastard's passing and his attempt to seek absolution. The chaplain even brought the Bible the Old Bastard had been holding on to him.

He placed it on my bedside and I told him there was no use. I if there was a God, he didn't come to my chamber then and surely wouldn't now.

The chaplain prayed, but God never showed up. We both knew these actions meant the end of my run on Earth. I would get to pay my respects soon and then others would hopefully pay me mine. I could hear the families of the rats in my head as my carcass was lowered into the ground.

"It's ironic that a bastard who's lived a life tormenting others looks so peaceful. I don't understand, after all these years, how he can lie there so fragile. His actions have been anything but that. His ability to shape and mold horrific scenes behind closed doors are now lost to time and hopefully hell, too. The world was oblivious. His friends were oblivious. His co-workers; oblivious. His external family; unconcerned. All of them were too busy with their own personal shit-shows to realize the nightmare he was unleashing in this city. No matter the amount of pain he unleashed on this world, he still gets to rest. It's not fair. None of it. Throw the dirt on the son-of-a-bitch. Time stops for no man. Not even this bastard."

Currently nestled between cornfields and the majestic Wabash River in southern Indiana, James Watjen spends his days honing his craft as a writer and filmmaker while cherishing precious moments with his wife and three wonderful children.

His journey as a storyteller has been deeply influenced by a lifelong fascination with the thriller and horror genres, with masters of the craft like Stephen King, George Romero, and William Lustig serving as the backbone of his inspiration. It's from this talented and amazing group of storytellers that he draws his greatest inspirations. Whether it be through the classic novels of King or the psychological and unhinged works of Romero and Lustig, the influence is sometimes subtle yet present.

James is currently working through several original and disturbing releases for the next few years.

ALSO AVAILABLE FROM
NIGHTMARE PRESS

In Dormancy, They Sleep by D.G. Sutter

While vacationing in Gloucester, Massachusetts with his wife, a journalist named Paul stumbles upon the big break he's been seeking. On a kayaking trip just off New England's infamous North Shore, Paul hears the story of young Daniel Fogle – the boy who went missing years ago while exploring underground caverns.

Paul becomes obsessed with unraveling Fogle's mysterious disappearance: A case the town of Gloucester has long kept a secret. Tracing the aged footsteps the boy left behind, Paul finds himself in the same lair that changed young Daniel's life, encountering an otherworldly horror he could never have imagined, and placing him in a fight for his life, the town of Gloucester, and the very fabric of our world.

From the mythical Dogtown to Hammond Castle, to the breakwater and Eastern Point Lighthouse, *In Dormancy, They Sleep* is a modern folktale about fabricated myths, torn relationships, and conspiracy, with plenty of classic creature terror!

All Roads Lead by Jennifer Winters

A teenage girl visiting relatives wonders if her young cousin is just the spoiled baby of the family, or something worse? Something dark and devouring latches onto a young widow's grief. A lonely young woman tells her haunting story of finding love and family.

Welcome to Rhodes: a lovely, small town that is so pleasant it's scary.

All Roads Lead brings you a collection of stories that will take you down different roads that may seem familiar, but take dark turns along the way to carry you into the territories of nightmares, monsters, and mystery.

The Untaken by Bekki Pate

They're in her room again. She watches them glide silently closer. She closes her eyes against the threat of their presence. Long, bony hands roam her body. It's happening again, and again there's nothing she can do about it. There's a bright flash of light, and they take her.

Charlie Samuels is an abductee. She's used to that now, never knowing anything different, and she's almost in control of most parts of her life. But a new threat appears, something made from nightmares, something designed to target people like her.

Charlie soon finds herself wrapped up in a conspiracy much bigger than she ever imagined, and the beings she has spent her entire life running away from may have been on her side all along.

The Cursed Diary of a Brooklyn Dog Walker by Michael Reyes

There's something strange going on in Brooklyn. Occult chants ring out in the dead of night from quaint brownstones and trendy coffee shops. The stench of blood-soaked orgies and human sacrifice wafts through yoga studios and food co-ops. The servants of the demon star have come to power. And they are hunting for the only soul that can destroy them.

Whoops! I Woke the Dead by Joseph Rubas

Alex Warner was just your average sixteen-year-old gal – wait, no she wasn't. Alex Warner was the coolest person to ever live. She had a hot, dorky boyfriend, a nerdy little sister who was actually her cousin, and a book – a really gnarly old book made from human skin. But you see, that's right up Alex's alley, because not only is she completely awesome, with her job at Pissy's Pizza, her volunteer work at the library, and her VSCO friend who gives everyone scrunchies, but she also loves Halloween. And this book is perfect for this year's witch costume. Only…it's not a costume book, and when she reads it aloud in the graveyard…

Whoops! I Woke the Dead!

…sorry.

Butchers (Vampire Series of Extreme Horror #01) by Todd Sullivan

Kidnapped, turned, and locked away in a concrete basement, high school student Sey-Mi is taught the ways of the damned. Her captors – beautiful and malignant, cruel and insane – torture her until she pledges allegiance to the Gwanlyo: a secret organization of vampires now obsessed with bringing her into their ranks.

Enter rouge members Cheol Yu and Hyeri, who want to liberate vampires and set them upon humankind like a plague. Their first act of rebellion is to persuade Sey-Mi to join them in their twisted objective of unraveling this draconian society of the dead. Before they can do that, they will have to dodge the Natural Police, an order within the Gwanlyo whose objective is to hunt down and butcher any vampires that break the organization's strict rules, and who are currently tracking Cheol Yu for murdering one of their own.

Hyeri, who is no stranger to the organization's wicked methods of agonizing punishment, is hell-bent on bringing them down, and is prepared to lead Cheol Yu through the dark, abandoned streets of the Gwanlyo's compound where Sey-Mi is being held captive. She doesn't intend to go in unarmed, however. Hyeri has a plan – one that might just burn the Gwanlyo to the ground.

Will Sey-Mi place her loyalties in the Gwanlyo that rules through terror? Will she side with rebellious conspirators who strive to bring hell to the world? Or will she carve out her own path through the flesh and bone of anyone who stands in her way? Find out in Butchers: a novella of extreme horror.

The Gray Man of Smoke and Shadows (_Vampire Series of Extreme Horror #02_) by **Todd Sullivan**

When she was a child, Hyeri's uncle tortured her. Years after escaping his brutal touch, she discovers a secret organization of vampires and joins the ranks of the undead. Gaining supernatural strength and speed, she seeks one thing: revenge.

When Hyeri unleashes her decades-old hatred upon her uncle, she's interrupted by a vampire enforcer who seeks to apprehend her for breaking company protocol and revealing her vampiric nature to mortals.

Hyeri fends off the assassin, but an errant attack wounds her uncle, and the vampires glimpse an evil that has taken refuge inside of him. The darkness desires to remain unknown and plots to silence them both. Forced to combine their abilities, the vampire duo sharpen their swords and gorge on blood to increase their strength.

Can they withstand the onslaught of Hyeri's uncle: The Gray Man of Smoke and Shadows?

Before they can find out, someone else stumbles onto their path. Someone with abilities they have never seen. This strange being, full of rage and vengeance, is hell-bent on destruction. But who will be his target?

Find out in Volume II of the _Vampire Series of Extreme Horror_ based in South Korea.

Chainsaw Sisters **by Jacob Floyd**

When Sis wakes up in her father's backyard, staring at a rickety old shed, she can't remember how she got there or even who she is. But she remembers Amy, the sister that disappeared long ago, the same sister that she now hears calling to her from the shed.

When Sis enters the shed she discovers that Amy is only there in spirit, and she is speaking to her through a new body, and that body just happens to be a chainsaw.

Amy reveals to Sis that she was murdered by a local crime ring and she needs Sis to seek revenge for her. Sis agrees to the task and as Amy guides her to the home of each man responsible, Sis uses Amy's new body to hack them to pieces.

But the situation isn't as straightforward as it seems at first. As Sis comes face to face with each man, she finds herself in the middle of unfamiliar flashbacks that put her at the scene of a heinous crime of which she has no recollection. In time, she begins to believe that these are not her memories and Amy isn't telling her everything she needs to know.

What lies ahead beyond the coming bloodbath is something darker and more disturbing than Sis could have imagined.

Who is Amy?
Who is Sis?
And what connection do they both have to the men she's about to murder?

Bella by Michael Conley

In an alternate 1800's America, where magic is real and dragons soar through the skies of the American frontier, Topher had a good life, mostly. It wasn't great, but what can a young African girl expect living on the Edge of the World?

She had a shack that she shared with her Ma, she knew what vendors she could pocket an apple from, and was better than anyone with a spitshot. What more could a girl in the slums expect?

Then that chucklehead Wasco rolled out of the mountains like a toppled boulder. Topher had figured he might be good for a penny or two if she showed him around. Before she knew it he had her trompin' around the Blacklands, getting shot at, almost eaten and damn near gutted by some bull-headed dandy!

Jacob, who was about the handsomest gunfighter a body could imagine, might be some kind of monster. Old Ying turned out to be one of them wizards from the storybooks and Li had a magic sword!

All because someone went and took Bella and Wasco aimed to get her back, and Topher had been too stubborn not to follow him.

Yeah, it had been a good enough life. She just wasn't sure she was going to make it back to it, or if she even wanted to.

Night of the Possums by Jacob Floyd

The night of the possums began on a chilly autumn morning around 2am in late October.

On a dark country road, a young man is torn to shreds by wild animals. The news of his grisly death rocks the town. When a similar death occurs later that day, the town is in the grips of fear.

In rural Bardstown, Kentucky, opossums have risen up against the populace. People are being maimed and devoured throughout the city. These are not your ordinary opossums, either: They are smarter, stronger, faster, and far more vicious—some larger than any opossum anyone has ever seen, growing as long as four feet and as heavy as fifty pounds, with teeth capable of cleaving bone.

As the flesh-eating scourge quickly spreads from one end of Bardstown to the other, a few of those who survived the attacks band together in an attempt to eradicate the maniac marsupials. But, the number of the beasts grows by the hour and the force becomes too insurmountable; the survivors soon realize escape is their only option.

But, beyond the berserk behavior of the carnivorous creatures is a darker secret—something ancient and unnatural that threatens all those who are bitten and live to tell about it.

Before anyone can find out what is driving these opossums to kill, the survivors must battle their way through the merciless onslaught of claws and teeth and leave the threat of Bardstown behind them.

ANTHOLOGIES FROM NIGHTMARE PRESS

Animal Uprising!

A lion, a hybrid, a bear – oh no! A goat, a gull, and a big black dog! Can't forget the roaches, the deer flies, and the tarantula hawk, or the abominable insect that rises from the earth! We got creepy crawlers and killer critters for everyone. Oh, you want mythical creatures? How about a malevolent spirit posed as a fox, a rambunctious jackalope, or a herd of unicorn-gazelles on a distant planet? Let's not forget the supernatural silver stag with the power to raise the dead. Oh, did I mention the giant mantis shrimp? Yeah – we got a giant mantis shrimp. Humankind really has their work cut out for them in this collection of terrifying tales of beastly butchery. Need to know more? Check out *Animal Uprising!* for all of the mayhem.

Retro Horror

Welcome, ladies and gentleman, to Retro Horror…
Where monsters battle for supremacy; where the hand of evil touches all; where one gets lost in their own madness.

Remember when horror used to keep you up at night as it flickered from your television set, packed with ghouls, ghosts, demons, and madmen? Well, we have many late-night terrors for you, dear reader, if you dare to turn these pages. We have water monsters, trees with eyes, cryptid creatures, and hybrid horrors. Be prepared to face reanimated bodies, mad scientists, and barbarous butchers. If you're not afraid to face the horrible beasts and frightening fiends herein, sit back and get ready because Retro Horror has arrived.

Todd Sullivan Presents: The Vampire Connoisseur

But like all of us, Vinson delivered the dead bodies he created to our parasites, the imps; bodies for disposal which would otherwise rot in plain sight of Mankind, be pondered and investigated. Exposed corpses were too dangerous for us, a tiny minority stalking the world of fragile mortals. Buried bodies were discovered too often. And new technology? iPhones with cameras, still shots or videos uploaded for eternity on the internet highway revealed us to the billions of spiteful people on the planet, the villagers with pitchforks. – "Parasites: A Tale of Route 66"

The Dark Frontier

There's something sinister in the mountain, letting monsters loose upon the world. Civilization is collapsing; the lands are submerged in shadow. Soon, the darkness will consume the countryside, leaving but one path through the void – a path that cuts across the Dark Frontier.

This western wasteland sprawls across the ruins of what were once the great cities of humankind. Now, beneath the looming devastation, standing on the precipice of extinction, man finds himself driven by temptation and survival to steal and to kill. The innocent huddle in the shades and crevices of civilization's cemetery, praying to the deafened gods of faded faiths to help them make it through the apocalypse. Then the dark guardians of the new world rise from the deep, stomping over the land, and feeding on the twisted souls of those who survived the first cataclysm.

In its last stand for survival, humanity will tear itself into fragments and then scatter in the winds of war, famine, and fire. Regimes meant to protect the populace, lone heroes, and those determined to make it through the end times will rise and fall, live and die, and cross the broken prairies and scorched lands only to arrive in cities reduced to rubble, crawling with killers and creatures that devour the ghosts of man. They will have no choice but to return to the shattered wilderness of the Dark Frontier.

It is out there, beyond the edges of dead worlds, past the graveyards where the grand plans of man now wither and rot, where all shall find their end, where humanity's swan song will be swallowed by the black winds of chaos spreading from the hills and mountains. Trapped in the shadows that surround the world, as the wall of the black void closes in, man's revelation comes down to one question: is the evil out there where the world is dying, or was the Dark Frontier inside us all along?

The Pale Horse has come, and it carries the Black Angel. Get ready to ride.

PARANORMAL NONFICTION FROM NIGHTMARE PRESS

Kentucky's Strange and Unusual Haunts by The Frightening Floyds

The Bluegrass State is home to many haunted legends. Stories of witches, ghosts, demons, monsters, "black things", "white thangs", and even headless horsemen abound across Kentucky. In this book you will read nearly a hundred of those legends taken from all across the state. From the hilltop of Western Kentucky University to the classy Seelbach Hotel, from the infamous Bobby Mackey's Music World to the notorious Waverly Hills Sanatorium, you'll read tales about hotels, schools, landmarks, graveyards, mountains, hills, tunnels, lonely roads, and many other locations including the historic Mammoth Cave. So if you're in for a good scare, sit back with the Frightening Floyds and learn all about *Kentucky's Strange and Unusual Haunts*.

Strange and Unusual Mysteries by The Frightening Floyds

What you are about to read is not a news report; it is neither a bulletin nor an alert. Rather, it is a collection of accounts of strange and unusual occurrences – some solved, some unsolved, but all mysterious. These reports have circulated for decades; some so much that they have become the sources of legends and rumors, even theories involving deep conspiracies. Despite many investigations and countless hours of research, there remain many questions unanswered. However, for every mystery there is someone out there who knows the truth, who possesses the evidence to solve the riddle. Maybe that someone will open this book and find their report. That someone could even be you.

Ahead you will find tales of ghosts, missing persons, ancient legends, and extraterrestrial visitors. What are their stories, or, more importantly, where did their stories come from? Read the enclosed accounts and decide for yourself.

Please, join us – maybe you can help the Frightening Floyds solve a mystery.

American Cryptic **by Jim Towns**
AMERICAN CRYPTIC is an open-minded cynic's take on the uncanny and sometimes frightening things which border our accepted reality. Through thirteen stories and essays, author and filmmaker Jim Towns examines several legends native to his own roots in Western Pennsylvania, and recalls some of his own unexplainable experiences as well. From legends of Native American giants buried under great earth mounds, to a haunted asylum, to a phantom trolley passenger, this work seeks not only to present the reader with new and fascinating supernatural tales, but also to deconstruct why our culture is so fascinated by their telling and re-telling.

Handbook for the Dead
DON'T FORGET YOUR HANDBOOK…

Welcome all spirits! The Frightening Floyds present to you, *Handbook for the Dead* – a guide to help all new manifestations realize their functional perimeters.

Within this anthology, you'll read paranormal accounts from individuals who have experienced phantoms and disturbances that have not only chilled them, but also left them with some new insight into the supernatural. Now, they want to share their stories and wisdom with you. That way, if you're feeling a little flat, or even if you're a lost soul, you won't have to draw a door and knock.

Handbook for the Dead is sure to please the strange and unusual in everyone, and we promise it doesn't read like stereo instructions.

<u>*Aliens Over Kentucky*</u> by The Frightening Floyds

From the Frightening Floyds, the pair of paranormal enthusiasts who brought you *Be Our Ghost* and *Haunts of Hollywood Stars and Starlets* comes a new adventure into the realm of the unknown – *Aliens over Kentucky*.

This collection includes the most noted extraterrestrial encounters from the Bluegrass State, such as the Kelly Creatures Incident of 1955, the Stanford Abductions, the Dogfight above General Electric, and the tale of Capt. Thomas Mantell chasing a UFO through Kentucky skies. But that's not all. There are lesser known, but equally intriguing, reports herein, such as the train collision with the UFO, stories of unexplained crop circles and cattle mutilations, Spring-heeled Jack, the Meat Shower of 1876, and many eyewitness reports of various unidentified crafts. You'll also read a couple of personal experiences from the authors, and even Muhammad Ali gets involved in the alien action.

Join Jacob and Jenny Floyd as they dig into the mysterious cases and theories regarding Kentucky's "X-Files". Just be sure to keep one eye on the book and the other on the sky...

Be Our Ghost by The Frightening Floyds
The Frightening Floyds invite you to be our ghost as we take you on a tour of the happiest haunted place on Earth! In this book, you will read about much of the alleged paranormal activity as well as urban legends spanning the various Disney theme parks around the world. From the haunted dolls of It's a Small World to the real ghosts of the Haunted Mansion, there are many spirits here to greet you. And make sure to say "Good morning" to George at Pirates of the Caribbean.

Enjoy the spooky and fascinating tales in *Be Our Ghost*! And don't worry, there are no hitchhiking ghosts ahead...or are there?

Paranormal Encounters
The Frightening Floyds present *Paranormal Encounters*: a collection of 14 tales of true ghostly experiences. From a malevolent spirit remaining in an apartment, to a loving phone call from a lost relative; from a house with a sliding chair and slamming doors, to a snow globe moving across a bedroom; from a possible past-life

experience to a ghostly stranger in a radio station, this anthology contains several strange and unusual stories that are sure to entertain fans of the paranormal.

Haunts of Hollywood Stars and Starlets by The Frightening Floyds

Explore the dark side of Tinseltown in this collection of paranormal stories, conspiracy theories, curses, and legends about some of Hollywood's most iconic names: Marilyn Monroe, Rudolph Valentino, Charlie Chaplin, James Dean, Jean Harlow, Clark and Carole, Lucille Ball, Michael Jackson, Bela Lugosi, Lon Cheney, John Belushi, and the King himself—Elvis Presley—and many more. Join the Frightening Floyds as they take you on a terrifying journey through the city of glamour and glitz!

www.ingramcontent.com/pod-product-compliance
Lightning Source LLC
Chambersburg PA
CBHW052015170626
46808CB00007B/2943